D1493762

IMAGINE THAT

Licensed exclusively to Imagine That Publishing Ltd
Tide Mill Way, Woodbridge, Suffolk, IP12 1AP, UK
www.imaginethat.com
Copyright © 2020 Imagine That Group Ltd
All rights reserved
4 6 8 9 7 5 3
Manufactured in China

Written by Isabel Pope
Illustrated by Róisín Hahessy

All rights reserved. No part of this publication may be reproduced, stored in a retrieval system, or transmitted in any form or by any means, electronic, mechanical, photocopying, recording or otherwise, without the prior written permission of the publisher. Neither this book nor any part or any of the illustrations, photographs or reproductions contained in it shall be sold or disposed of otherwise than as a complete book, and any unauthorised sale of such part illustration, photograph or reproduction shall be deemed to be a breach of the publisher's copyright.

ISBN 978-1-78958-586-5

A catalogue record for this book is available from the British Library

How Much Do I Love You?

Written by Isabel Pope

Illustrated by Róisín Hahessy

How much do I love you,
my little one?

I love you as much
as the jungle ...

where the wild things are.

I Love you as deep as the ocean ...

where the whales swim far.

I Love you as high as the mountains ...

frozen white with icy snow.

I Love you as far as the night sky ...

where the moon and stars glow.

My heart is full of love for you ...

how I love you so.

I love you more than anything ...
more than you can know.